La Boca Twilight

Written by John Parsons
Illustrated by Linhan Ye

Contents

NELSON
CENGAGE Learning™
For learning solutions, visit cengage.com.au

Meet the Characters

Victor Ruiz

A young violin player.

Señor Florida

The owner of La Perla.

Eduardo

The bouncer at La Perla.

Señora Salguero

A once-famous tango dancer.

Dear Reader

Many years ago, I found myself in a cafe called La Perla in La Boca, Buenos Aires. Guarding the cafe's entrance was the scariest doorman I have ever seen. As soon as I laid eyes upon him, I knew he would appear in one

of my books. I hope you like this story – and, if I ever go back to La Boca, I hope the doorman likes it, too. Otherwise, I'm in big trouble!

John Parsons
Author

Buenos Aires

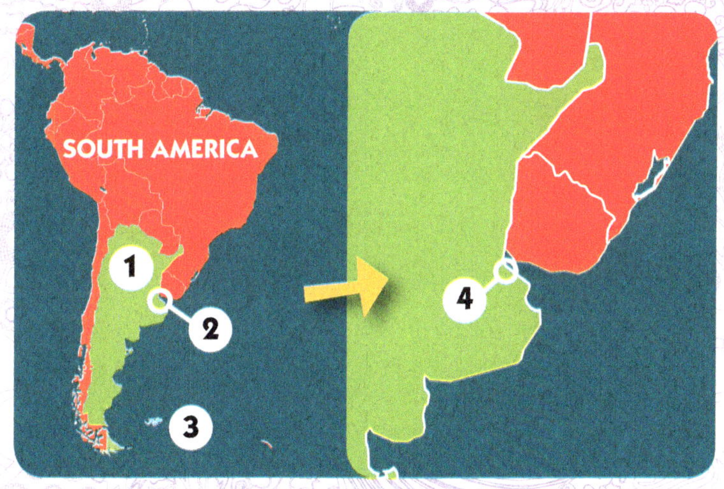

1. Argentina
2. Buenos Aires
3. Las Islas Malvinas
4. La Boca (a suburb of Buenos Aires)

1 A Wily Chameleon

Any good tourist guidebook will describe La Boca as a *barrio*, or neighbourhood, in the south-east of Buenos Aires, in Argentina, South America. What it won't describe are the slow, filthy waters of the Matanza River, better known as El Riachuelo, or "The Little River", with its rusting, half-submerged freighters, marking La Boca's southern boundary. To the east, the sullen river wharves are bullied by the surging, oily waters of the Rio Plata. To the west lies the grim working-class area of Barracas and the slums of Nueva Pompeya, known to the locals as *villa miseria* – the villages of misery.

To the tourist, the face of La Boca is Caminito, a colourful street market, where couples in elegant costume will dance the tango for ten pesos. Here, on hot, overcast Saturdays, throngs of tourists jostle for cheap T-shirts that later fall apart in their suitcases. To the ardent sports fan,

this *barrio* is home to a football team, the Boca Juniors, source of hope and crushing despair to thousands of fervent supporters resplendent in colours of blue and yellow. To the weary taxi driver, it is a fifty-peso fare from downtown Buenos Aires, never to be accepted on game day. To the residents, La Boca is a living thing, a wily chameleon that creeps slowly along a precarious twig, its skin changing colour by the hour. It has a thousand eyes, flickering, watching, hungry for prey. Find yourself lost in this *barrio* and it will swallow you in a second.

To Victor Ruiz, a hopeful young musician from the vast Argentinean countryside, La Boca was a destination often dreamed about, but not yet reached.

On his first afternoon in Buenos Aires, Victor had three duties to fulfil: to his family, his country and to himself.

Travelling south through the city, with his small backpack and violin case, Victor stopped first at the Plaza San Martin, near the main ports of the city. There, he set himself the solemn task of finding his grandfather's name on the wall commemorating those who had died in Argentina's invasion of Las Islas Malvinas, an ill-fated attempt to recapture the disputed islands from the British thirty years before.

Amongst the hundreds of names, he soon found that of Manuel Ruiz. He ran his fingers across the letters carved into the smooth black stone. He had never met his grandfather – a British missile fired to protect the islands they knew as the Falklands had seen to that – but he had heard the tales of his bravery.

Victor sat for a few minutes beneath his grandfather's name, trying in his heart to feel sadness or loss. But the sounds of the city drowned out his thoughts and, although he did his best to silently pay his respects, a name carved on a wall could not evoke a real person. The late afternoon sun was hot and drained his spirits. He stood and started to walk south. His first duty left him feeling faintly hollow but was, nevertheless, complete.

After an hour, Victor found himself at the Plaza de Mayo, a dusty square hemmed in by tired government buildings and dominated by the faded presidential palace, Casa Rosa. This square marked his country's birthplace and was, for many Argentineans, the heart of their country.

From the palace balcony overlooking the square, the famous Evita and her husband, the steely Argentinean president Juan Peron, had once waved at crowds of patriotic followers. When their popularity waned, the square transformed itself into the scene of violent protests and riots. As the mood of the country rose and fell, so too did the passion of the people who came to stand amongst the watchful statues and plaques of the Plaza de Mayo. Today, there were only small clusters of curious tourists and a handful of stray dogs lazing in the sunshine.

As Victor tried, and failed, to imagine the passion that had flared here throughout the years, a military band filed out of the Casa Rosa. Out of step and looking bored, they finally arrived at the flagpole in the plaza and assembled themselves in a formation. While one of the soldiers tried to untangle the knotted lanyard around the flagpole, the band struck up a patriotic tune. But, instead of being stirring, it was flat and out of step, like the band's half-hearted marching. The local stray dogs, their afternoon sleep disturbed, embarked upon their own impromptu performance, howling and barking. Finally, the soldier at the base of the flagpole released the lanyard, and the limp blue and white flag, emblazoned with a multi-pointed sun, was lowered to a dull cacophony of brass, drums and dogs.

The tourists drifted away, the dogs fell back on their sides, and Victor walked to a corner of the square, his eyes scanning the avenue for a black and yellow taxi. Vaguely disappointed, he had nonetheless completed his second duty, and he could continue his journey south. With the sun falling and the changing moods of the *barrios* between here and his destination, he knew a taxi was the safest option.

He flagged down a taxi and, with relief, saw the small blue and yellow beads hanging from the driver's rear-view mirror. This driver would not refuse a fare to his football team's home *barrio*.

Victor climbed in, clutching his violin case and backpack. He hoped his third duty would be more satisfying.

"La Boca," he said. Without a word, the driver joined the rush-hour traffic creeping around the square that marked the weary heart of Buenos Aires.

2 La Perla

A pair of alarmingly bloodshot eyes, ringed with dark smudges, examined Victor sceptically. The owner of the eyes, a man so huge he filled the doorway of the cafe, grunted. "Wait here," he breathed. The man squeezed his bulk through the doorway and disappeared into the gloom.

Victor stood outside, looking at the peeling paint and grimy windows of La Perla. Once, this place had indeed been a pearl, famous throughout Buenos Aires and beyond for its beauty. But years of dust and decay had removed all remnants of its lustrous surface. Victor did not care. To the musician in him, the outside did not matter – he wanted to taste the stale air inside, to stand on the stage, to run his hands over the velvet curtains, to breathe in the atmosphere. This was La Perla. From the 1920s until the '50s, appreciative crowds had filled La Perla to hear the soulful music of the tango legends echo from its walls and fill the streets and alleyways of La Boca. It had been the most famous music venue in all of Argentina. This was the third, and most compelling, reason Victor had come to Buenos Aires.

The looming shadow of the bouncer filled the doorway again. A huge finger beckoned and, with a smile, Victor entered the place of his dreams.

The bouncer waved Victor over to a table and, with a parting glare, returned to barricade the doorway. A wrinkled man sat at the table, pouring sachet after sachet of sugar into a chipped cup of coffee.

"Who are you?" asked the man, stirring the black, syrupy coffee.

"Victor Ruiz," replied the young musician. "I have come from Santa Carmel, where I am a musician. A tango musician."

"I've never heard of it," replied the old man, keeping his eyes on the coffee before him. "I've never heard of you."

"I am the winner of our provincial championship for violin," said Victor proudly. "Our local newspaper described me as a violinist with promise."

The old man snorted and he fixed Victor with a scornful expression. "A violinist with promise from a town I've never heard of in a province I don't care about. What do you want?"

"I'd like to audition to play at La Perla," said Victor.

"We already have a tango band," sighed the old man wearily. He sipped his coffee.

"Will you at least listen to my playing? I have brought my violin," said Victor.

"I don't need a violin player," repeated the old man. "Eduardo!"

The bouncer's frame blocked out the last remaining daylight. "Yes, Señor Florida?" he growled.

"Victor Ruiz is leaving," said the old man.

"Please, señor, may I play just one tune? Even if you don't want me, just to play one tune in La Perla has been a dream of mine for ..."

Somewhere in the darkness, a phone rang. Señor Florida waved at Eduardo to take the call.

"It would mean so much to me, señor," pleaded Victor. "I just want to experience the atmosphere, the sounds, the excitement."

Eduardo put down the phone and leant down to whisper in Señor Florida's ear.

"A broken jaw?" the old man grumbled. "I pay him to pour coffee, not talk to the customers. If he hasn't broken his arms or his hands, why can't he come in to work?"

Eduardo shrugged his massive shoulders, and the old man exhaled in irritation. "Now I am a waiter short. What will I do? Serve them myself?"

Eduardo leant down again, and the old man's eyes narrowed. He nodded and turned to Victor.

"If you want to experience the atmosphere and the sounds of La Perla, you are in luck. I will allow you to serve coffee for one night only. But you'd better hope there's no excitement. Last night's excitement has left me short-staffed."

Victor's face split into a huge smile. "Thank you, señor," he said. "Thank you, thank you."

"I will not pay you. A night at La Perla will be your reward," said Señor Florida gruffly.

Throughout the afternoon, Victor had felt his enthusiasm for Buenos Aires slowly draining away. At Plaza San Martin and Plaza de Mayo, the sadness and the pride he had expected to feel had been disappointingly absent. But, in the dark and dingy interior of La Perla, with the offer of a night's work in the venue of his dreams, his spirits started to lift. He looked around at the faded carpets, the scuffed and battered furniture, the grimy chandeliers, and saw only a glorious history, a place that for generations of musicians, dancers and patrons had been radiant with the promise of beauty.

"Put your precious violin behind the bar," added Señor Florida. "You won't need it." He finished his coffee with a satisfied slurp. "You might need your fists, though."

3 A Faded Legend

That night, the patrons of La Perla were subdued. Beneath the old chandeliers, the cafe took on a different ambience, shadows hiding the stains and faded interior. Like Victor, no one looked at the décor. Instead, they watched the stage.

Victor was waiting for the barista to finish making a round of coffees when he noticed the old lady. She slipped past Eduardo, who acknowledged her presence with his customary grunt. She selected a table at the rear of the cafe. Señor Florida nodded at her respectfully and was rewarded with a nod in return.

Victor's attention returned to the coffees. He carefully balanced the frothy glasses on his tray and was about to ferry them over to a table of patrons, when he heard a whisper at his back.

"*Café con leche* for Señora Salguero," hissed Señor Florida. "Make sure it's milky. And it's on the house."

Victor glanced over at the old lady in wonder. Señora Salguero. Surely she couldn't be *the* Señora Salguero? But then he was at La Perla. Perhaps it was.

"Is that ...?" he started, but Señor Florida had already walked away. Victor finished balancing the glasses of coffee and carried them over to their destination before hurrying back to the bar to order Señora Salguero's coffee with milk.

"Is that *the* Señora Salguero?" he asked the barista, who shrugged his shoulders with disinterest. He only cared about coffee, not tango. The name meant nothing to him. Victor waited for the milky coffee, placed it in the middle of his tray, and then walked over to the old lady's table.

"*Café con leche*," he said with a smile. The old lady kept her eyes on the band, which had just taken the stage. Victor decided to take a chance. "Señora Salguero, I am a great admirer. Your tango dancing is legendary, señora."

Señora Salguero's watery blue eyes flicked towards Victor. "Legends are only for those who live in the past, young man."

"But in the forties and fifties, you danced with the greats, señora," said Victor.

The old lady fixed Victor with an irritated frown. "No, young man, I did not. You are mistaken." Her attention returned to the stage.

Victor felt his face turning red with embarrassment. "Excuse me, señora. I thought you were someone else."

The old lady carried on as if she had not heard Victor's mumbled apology.

"I *was* one of the greats," she declared. "Other men danced with *me*."

Victor was about to reply when a long, soulful violin note echoed off the darkened walls and a chord from a *bandoneón* concertina rose to meet it.

"Shh," whispered the old lady, "the band is about to begin."

Despite Señor Florida's warnings, Victor did not need his fists that evening, only his hands to carry coffees. He was busy throughout the night, and he found satisfaction in every moment. He might not have been playing his violin up on stage, but he, Victor, a promising violinist from Santa Carmel, was at last in his element. He was at La Perla, sharing a night of soaring tango music with the legendary Señora Salguero. And then, all too soon, it finished.

The band left the stage and Victor headed towards Señora Salguero's table. He found himself blocked halfway by Señor Florida, who was pointing at the glasses littering the empty tables.

"What are you waiting for, Victor?" he demanded. "There are tables to clear. Hurry up."

Señora Salguero slipped past Eduardo and disappeared into the night alone. Victor had missed his chance. Instead, he busied himself clearing empty coffee glasses and rearranging tables and chairs.

“Where are you staying?” asked Señor Florida, when the cafe was ready to close.

“I thought I would head back into the city and find a hostel,” said Victor. “I can’t afford a hotel room.”

Señor Florida looked at his watch and then at Victor in disbelief. “At this time of night? You’re going back into the city?”

Victor nodded.

“*Insensato*,” muttered Señor Florida, shaking his head at Victor’s foolishness. He walked over to where Eduardo was guarding the door and murmured a few words. Eduardo looked over at Victor, and then nodded reluctantly at his boss. He squeezed his way past the tables and chairs and pushed Victor unceremoniously towards the back of the stage, where he pointed to a roll of blankets next to a camp stretcher.

“The camp stretcher’s mine,” he growled. “Grab a blanket and sleep on the stage.”

Victor’s first two duties had been less than satisfying, and his third had not turned out the way he had expected. Nevertheless, he had spent the night at La Perla in distinguished tango company. Now he was about to make it onto Argentina's most revered stage.

"You might still need your fists," hissed Señor Florida, as he completed the last of his checks. He nodded at Eduardo. "Thieves around here work in gangs, and my night guard can only handle three or four at a time. You will have to stop the rest yourself."

4 Tango on the Street

Victor never asked and Señor Florida never agreed. It just worked out that, as long as the young musician turned up, there were always coffees for him to deliver and, as long as he helped clear the empty tables at night, there was always a bed on the stage.

After a week, Señor Florida handed over a crumpled hundred-peso note without a word of explanation. He carried on talking to Eduardo, who was sweeping the night's dust and flakes of old paint out into the alleyway. After two weeks, Victor grew to realise he was becoming part of La Perla and its odd collection of characters.

He was no longer intimidated by the gruff, scowling Eduardo. He was careful, but not scared. He knew to stay well out of his way when he was in a darker mood than usual, and he knew not to attempt conversation with the huge man until he had finished his first cup of coffee in the morning.

During the day, Señor Florida seemed not to care if he disappeared for a few hours, so Victor spent that time practising his violin on a park bench near Caminito. Anxious tourists who had somehow strayed away from the relative safety of the bustling stalls and brightly coloured houses sometimes left him a few pesos in return for directions back to the main street. Others thought he was a busker, and listened for a few minutes before they became aware of their surroundings and hurried back to the security of the busier roads. The homeless ignored him, retreating inside their sidewalk shacks of cardboard and plastic, and other local residents walked past with scarcely a glance. His music was just another few bars in the noisy, rumbling score that rose from the dirty streets of La Boca.

While Victor had lost his fear of Eduardo, he remained nervous around the faded tango dancer, Señora Salguero. Each night, she took up the same

position, alone at the table, sipping milky *café con leche* and watching the band. Finally, he worked up the nerve to ask the old lady what he'd been wanting to for days.

"Señora Salguero," he smiled, placing another glass of coffee on her table. He had carefully waited for a break in the tango performance so she would not be distracted. "You know I am a great fan. I am also a violin player, one with promise, so they say. Would you do me the honour of perhaps listening to me one day?"

The old lady sipped her fresh glass of coffee. "Why?" she asked eventually.

"You are Señora Salguero. You have danced to the greatest tango musicians who ever lived. I would like your opinion on my playing," replied Victor.

"How do I know you are not trying to lure me to some desolate location, perhaps to rob me or kidnap me?" she demanded.

Victor thought for a moment. "You could tell Eduardo where you are going," he suggested.

"Very well," agreed Señora Salguero, after due consideration. "Where is your studio?"

Victor was taken aback. "I don't have one," he said. "I practise near the corner of Magallanes and Garibaldi, on the street."

"I will walk past at precisely two o'clock tomorrow," said the old lady. "If you are not there, I will not wait. It is not safe for a woman of my age to linger on the street. Now be quiet." She waved a hand at the stage. "The band is returning."

Señora Salguero was true to her word. At two o'clock the next day, Victor spotted her walking briskly along Garibaldi, head down, clutching her handbag. He smiled and, violin to his neck, drew back his bow to play the first notes of *Milonga Sentimental*, a classic tango piece. He, Victor, a promising violin player from Santa Carmel, was playing a recital for the legendary Señora Salguero. His fingers moved along the neck of his violin, and long, clear notes rose above the industrial clatter of La Boca. He glanced upwards, to gauge Señora Salguero's response, and was startled to see her still walking determinedly towards the intersection with Magallanes. His bow stopped, half drawn across his strings. "Did she not see me?" he thought in surprise. "How could she not hear my violin?"

That evening, as Señora Salguero took her usual seat in La Perla, Victor hurried over. "Señora Salguero," he said, a worried note in his voice. "Why didn't you stop and listen this afternoon?"

"I said I would walk past at precisely two o'clock," replied the old lady. "Did you not see me?"

"Well, yes, but I thought you would stop," murmured Victor. "I was performing *Milonga Sentimental* for you, señora."

"I did not say I would stop, young man," she replied, her watery eyes flicking upwards. "And you were not performing *Milonga Sentimental*. You were merely playing the required notes in the correct order."

Victor looked confused. The old lady sighed, and fixed him with a critical gaze.

"Technically, you may have promise," she conceded. "But you lack something – something much more important than mere notes."

"Señora?" said Victor, bewildered.

"A tango must be performed with heartstrings and violin strings," said Señora Salguero. "Without both, you have nothing."

Victor was crestfallen. He thought he had done well, but instead, he had disappointed. It was not the reaction he had expected.

"Señora, I ..." he started, but the old lady silenced him with a raised hand.

"Shh," she said, "the band is about to begin."

5 Trouble in the Air

Heartstrings. A week had passed, and yet the old lady's words still rang in Victor's ears. Angry at first, he gradually realised that she was right – but where did one find a tutor who could teach a musician, even one with promise, to pluck, bend and draw their bow across heartstrings?

It was not possible. Such things could not be taught. They could only be felt. They could only be discovered if one burrowed through year upon year of sadness and disappointment, loss and melancholy, and found a way to express them. Señora Salguero knew tango. She knew the secret. It was not music. It was emotion.

"Stop daydreaming," snapped Señor Florida. "It is game day and we will have a large crowd tonight. Get those tables set up."

Game day. Boca Juniors were playing at home, a few blocks west, and that meant after the final whistle, the restless crowds would spill out into the neighbouring streets and alleyways. Victor knew there would be trouble, even if the home team won. If they lost, there would be big trouble. He set about tidying the tables, while Eduardo stood like a rock in the doorway, the shadows under his eyes darker than usual, his scowl fixed. The hours ticked by as La Perla waited, with muted trepidation, for the night to fall.

After the first set, the band retired for a break. The cafe was noisy and full, and the barista was rushed off his feet. Victor hurried between the tables, collecting empty glasses and taking orders while Señor Florida moved around the cafe, ever watchful, waiting for the mood to change.

Victor, backing away from a table full of rowdy football fans, bumped into another patron, spilling his glass of coffee.

"Excuse me, señor, I am sorry," he said. He smiled apologetically. Señor Florida, alert to the slightest signal, glanced at Eduardo, who nodded imperceptibly and slowly closed the door. It had been four weeks since he had issued his warning to Victor. Four weeks, and Victor finally had to use his fists.

It was all over in seconds. Victor managed to duck the angry man's first swing, but not the second. He went flying backwards and smashed into another table of patrons. Dazed, he struggled to his feet, and attempted to throw a punch back at his attacker. He saw Eduardo, moving more swiftly than he could have imagined, thundering towards the altercation. The first table of patrons, four of them, stood up to join the scuffle. Eduardo seized two of them and banged their heads together. No sooner had they slumped back in their chairs than he lunged at another, the force of his massive body throwing the football fan off balance. The first man, the one Victor had inadvertently bumped into, was momentarily distracted and Victor's punch landed squarely on his face. Eduardo swung a gigantic fist and caught the remaining fan on the jaw. The man flew back, crashing into the band members who were sitting on the edge of the stage, transfixed by the spectacle. There was a cry of pain, and it was all over.

Eduardo stood in the middle of the cafe, panting like a dangerous boar, daring anybody to come close. The football fans lay dishevelled and bruised around him. The violin player from the band stood up, clutching his wrist, where the fourth of Eduardo's victims had fallen.

"*Café con leche*!" barked Señor Florida to Victor. He pointed to Señora Salguero's table.

She remained expressionless, staring resolutely at the stage, while coffee from an overturned glass slowly spread across her table.

Eduardo threw the troublemakers out into the street. Victor began to tremble, his nerves finally catching up to him. He steadied his hands, wiped Señora Salguero's table and went across to the bar to collect the coffee from the barista.

After a few hurried words with the band, Señor Florida walked over to the bar. "Remember I told you that you would not need your violin but that you might need your fists?" he growled to Victor.

"You were right, señor," said Victor, rubbing his bruised knuckles.

"I was wrong," snapped Señor Florida. He nodded towards the injured band member who was grimacing, holding his wrist. "One minute. The show must go on."

Victor stared at Señor Florida. "But, señor," he protested. "I am not ready. I must practise. I must prepare ..."

"One minute," hissed Señor Florida again. "I don't want this crowd getting unruly again!"

Nervously, Victor eyed the audience. Señora Salguero sat at her table, expectant. He remembered her words. Heartstrings. Emotion. He closed his eyes and burrowed deep within his soul, searching for sadness and melancholy. He thought about his grandfather, a life wasted, nothing but a forgotten name carved into a bleak wall. He thought of his once-proud country, reduced to faded glory and stray dogs. He thought of La Perla, a tattered remnant of the lustrous pearl she had once been. Focusing intently on his thoughts of loss, he used his bow to carve the first bars of *Milonga Sentimental* from his violin. His fingers danced along the neck of his instrument, and long, melancholy notes rose above the murmur of the audience, the hiss of the coffee machine and the clatter of glasses.

When the second set finished, he smiled, bowed and shook the hands of the other band members. He hurried over to Señora Salguero's table. She was standing up to leave.

"Señora?" he smiled hopefully.

Her watery blue eyes glanced up at Victor's expectant face. She shook her head. "Without both, you have nothing," she said, repeating her verdict from the week before.

Victor was crushed. He watched the old lady shuffle towards the doorway and slip past Eduardo and into the dark night. Outside, the chameleon that was La Boca lay hidden in the shadows, a thousand eyes, flickering, watching, hungry for prey.

6 Heartstrings and Emotion

Eduardo discovered Señora Salguero, collapsed against a filthy brick wall a few steps from La Perla. He put down his broom, and the flakes of pale paint he had swept up swirled back inside the cafe. Gently, he picked up Señora Salguero, cradled her in his massive arms and silently carried her back inside La Perla.

In the grey morning, the lights of the *ambulancia* cast an eerie blue glow through the cafe's dusty windows.

"She is still breathing," yawned a paramedic. "Maybe she fell, maybe she was pushed." He shrugged his shoulders. It had been a long night. Game night always was. "But it doesn't look good. An old lady like her, out all night ..." His voice trailed off and he shook his head.

"She may last another day in the hospital. Maybe two. Who knows?" said a second paramedic.

Victor was devastated. So this was how legends ended in La Boca – alone and in the darkness. The paramedics loaded the stretcher and its occupant into the back of the *ambulancia* and left without another word.

Victor could not face the remainder of the morning in the gloomy interior of La Perla. Instead, he wandered the streets of La Boca, eyes downcast, oblivious to the tourists, the hawkers, the homeless. He walked and he walked, until he came to a decision. He headed back to La Perla.

"Stop daydreaming," growled Señor Florida, when he stepped inside the dim cafe. "Get those tables set up."

"Señor Florida, I am going home," said Victor. "I came to Buenos Aires hoping to find ..." Victor struggled to find the words. What had he hoped to find? Like Señora Salguero, whatever dreams he had had lay broken, waiting for the inevitable.

"When you turned up here, I was a waiter short. I gave you a chance. Now I am a violin player short. What am I supposed to do? Play the notes myself?"

Victor didn't answer. He went behind the bar and retrieved his violin case. Suddenly, a huge palm slapped the case down onto the stained, chipped wood. Eduardo's black, swollen eyes glared at Victor.

"Tonight you play," he grunted. Victor looked at the bouncer and, for a second, he recalled his fear when he first laid eyes upon the scowling mountain of muscle.

La Perla would not let its odd collection of characters go that easily.

"One night," said Victor. "Then I go."

Victor telephoned the hospital that afternoon. The nurse he spoke to told him there'd been no bruising, no sign of violence. It seemed Señora Salguero had just collapsed, her frail old body slowly shutting down as the night grew colder. He knew from the nurse's voice he would never again have the chance to perform for the legendary tango dancer, to light up her eyes, to finally play with heartstrings and violin strings and to see her simply nod and say "yes".

That night, the patrons of La Perla were sparse and subdued. On stage, Victor saw nothing of the

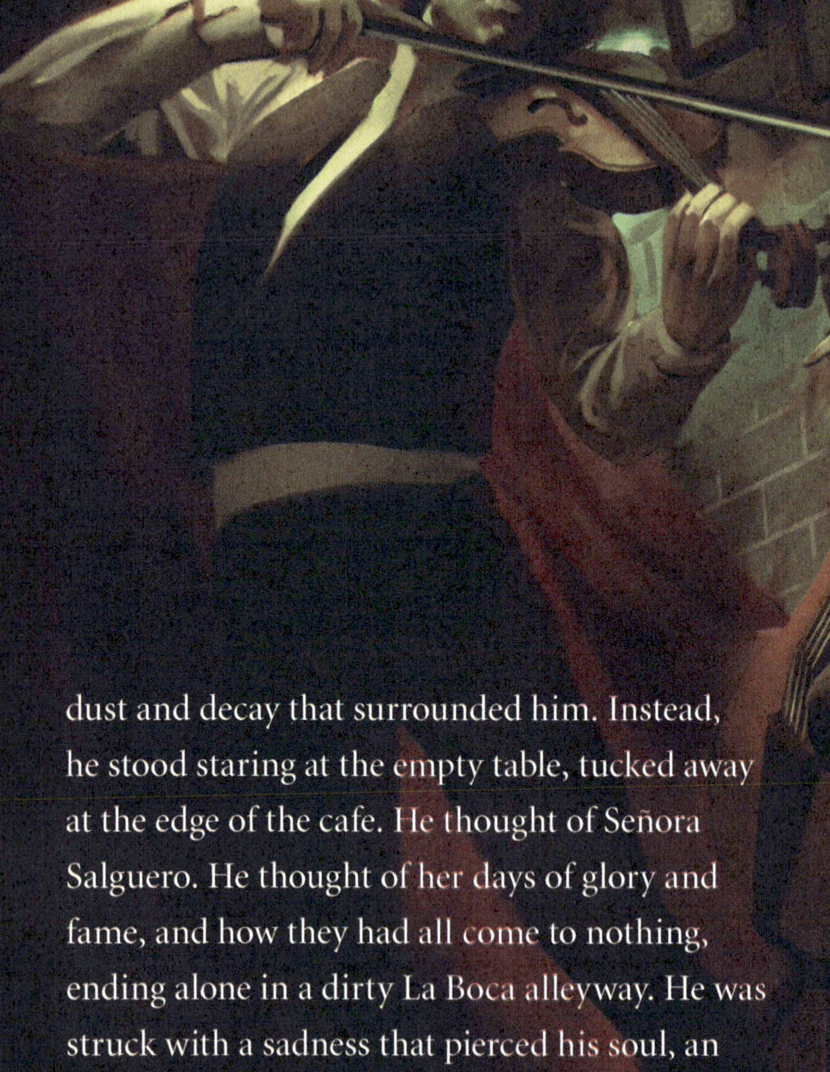

dust and decay that surrounded him. Instead, he stood staring at the empty table, tucked away at the edge of the cafe. He thought of Señora Salguero. He thought of her days of glory and fame, and how they had all come to nothing, ending alone in a dirty La Boca alleyway. He was struck with a sadness that pierced his soul, an emptiness that broke his heart.

He cradled his violin in the hollow of his shoulder and sighed deeply. A mournful note wailed across the meagre audience, and then another and another, each one wavering and climbing to reach its pitch.

Such things could not be taught. They could only be felt.

As the soaring notes echoed around the shadowy walls of La Perla, Victor did not notice the audience fall silent, fingers frozen around coffee glasses. No one moved.

Without both, you have nothing.

Victor continued, the tempo rising and falling. No one in the band dared attempt an accompaniment. Disconsolate, anguished notes sprang not from his fingers and bow, but from his despondent heart. Sadness and disappointment, loss and melancholy. Victor kept his eyes on the empty table at the back of the cafe. Señora Salguero had known tango. She had known the secret. And now she had gone. This was not music. It was emotion.

Finally, Victor finished his solo. He became aware of the audience clapping, and the noise broke the spell. He looked around at the faded carpets, the scuffed and battered furniture, the grimy, smoke-stained chandeliers.

Heartstrings and violin strings. Without both, you have nothing. But together, you find something unexpected. Victor bowed. He hoped Señora Salguero might have approved.

Señor Florida turned to Eduardo, whose frame filled the doorway. "Maybe he does have promise," he said. Eduardo just grunted. He stood motionless in the doorway, looking out over the chameleon that was La Boca. The slow, filthy waters of the Matanza River, better known as El Riachuelo, with its rusting, half-submerged freighters, ran to the south. Sullen wharves, bullied by the surging oily waters of the Rio Plata, lay to the east. To the west, the sun set behind the grim working class area of Barracas and the *villa miseria*.

The last of the sun's rays caught La Perla, dusty, decaying and tired. And for a moment, even to Eduardo's weary, dark eyes, it seemed to shine once more with a long-lost lustre.